The SQUiRReLS Who Squabbled

For Robbie — Bestest sharer of everything
in life (except chips) — R B

For our dear little Lola,
aka the Double Chinnais Guru.
Welcome to the World — J F

Text copyright © 2017 by Rachel Bright
Illustrations copyright © 2017 by Jim Field
First published in the United Kingdom in 2017 by Orchard Books London

ISBN 978-1-338-60600-3

10 9 8 7 6 5 4 3 2   19 20 21 22 23

Printed in the U.S.A.   141
First printing 2019

Rachel Bright

Jim Field

The SQUiRReLS Who Squabbled

Scholastic Inc.

In a towering forest, where summer had been,
The leaves turned to gold as a cold wind blew in,
And as autumn arrived with a sky raging red,
The sleepiest creatures got ready for bed.

While, up in a tree,
swung a flighty young squirrel,
Who everyone knew as
"Spontaneous Cyril."

Now, most foresty folk
had seen to their needs,
Through the plentiful months
of mushrooms and seeds.

They'd built up their stores
so they'd all be well fed
Through the frosting of winter
that glittered ahead.

But Cyril, he lived in the
NOW and the **HERE**.
He'd adventured and partied
his way through the year.

So his cupboard was empty,
his hollow was bare.

He hadn't a mouthful of
food **ANYWHERE**.

But WAIT! What was that?
Over there! Take a look!
A single lone pinecone,
wedged in a nook!
He squealed with delight —
and for very good reason . . .

For inside were the

Very.

Last.

Nuts.

Of.

The.

Season.

BUT . . . Cyril wasn't alone.
There were more hungry eyes.
Yes, "Plan-Ahead Bruce"
had his sights on the prize.

Though he'd gathered fresh treasures
Of *every* sort,
Bruce was convinced
he was ONE PINECONE SHORT.

"I simply MUST have it!"
he wistfully cried,
As he dreamt of the fresh,
juicy pine nuts inside.

So as Cyril set off
on his way to the ground,
Bruce, he was also
LAST-PINECONE- bound!

They sprinted and scurried —
with no time to gamble,
They scratched at the bark
in their scampering scramble.

But their panic and haste
shook the tips of the spruce,
And the pinecone,
it trembled and then . . .

IT CAME LOOSE!

Both squirrels gave
chase at a lightning pace.
This was the start of a
wild, nutty race . . .

"It's mine!" shouted Cyril.
"No, mine!" hollered Bruce . . .

"You don't stand a chance!
Give up! It's no use!"

"I'm HUNGRY!" cried Cyril.
"This cone is NOT yours!"

"Stay back!" shouted Bruce.
"This cone's for MY stores!"

It BOINGED over bushes . . . .

and flew through the air.

It BINGED on the nose of a slumbering bear!

It BOUNCED over boulders then came to a . . .

STOP.

Then teetered
and wobbled
and quivered
and . . .

PLOP!

Both squirrels followed.
Oh! The water was fast!
Would they learn that they needed
each other at last?

But EACH was intent
on how HE could win,
So they didn't quite notice
A BIRD SWOOPING IN!

Cyril and Bruce,

they watched in dismay,

As their cone disappeared up

up . . . UP . . . and AWAY!

"Come back!" shouted Cyril.

"They're our nuts!" exclaimed Bruce.

But all hope was gone.

It was simply no use.

And meanwhile they drifted
right up to the ledge.
Greed, it was driving them . . .

OVER THE EDGE.

Cyril and Bruce,
they had taken a fall.
They were paying the price
for wanting it all.

They'd squandered their chances
to team up and share.
Would their nutty young hopes
simply end in despair?

Bruised and bedraggled,
they swept past dry land.

Cyril grabbed at a branch
with a trembling hand.

Catching Bruce with the other, he heaved and he huffed . . .

And pulled him to safety, with panting and puffs.

They dragged themselves up with sputtering wriggles. Then Bruce looked at Cyril and . . .

Exploded in GIGGLES!

"How silly we are!"
he managed to mutter.
"How greedy I've been!"
he proclaimed with a splutter.

"We shall change from today.
May the squabbling cease.
We should celebrate — seeing
we're both in one piece!"

From that day and forward,
they made a great pair.
They would gather together
and found they COULD share.

Yes, Cyril and Bruce,

they knew in the end . . .

The BEST thing to share is
a laugh with your friend.